U.S. English Edition

Aliens Love Astronauts

TOW Gang Picture Books

4

Funny Bedtime Story -
Picture Book / Beginner Reader
About Making New Friends
(Ages 3-7)
by
Melinda Kinsman

To **Chris**

Wishing you a lifetime filled with fun, happiness and adventures!

ISBN-13: 978-1514815670

ISBN-10: 1514815672

1st Edition

Text and Illustrations

Copyright © Melinda Kinsman 2015

Printed by CreateSpace, an Amazon.com Company

Meet the
Top of the Wardrobe Gang

We're a team of cuddly toys who love writing for kids. We hope you enjoy our book.

Zog's Camouflage Challenge

This is Zog. He is the aliens' pet.

P.D.Monkey has drawn him in every picture. Can you find him?

Tip - Zog can change his colors to look like his surroundings, and he loves hiding!

Aliens LOVE astronauts,
and here's the reason why...
They find their BOOTS delicious –
both as snacks, or in a pie!

The grown-ups like the blue boots,
while the youngsters all want red.
Their noble king and queen
prefer the silver ones instead.

The astronauts all landed
in a very large tin can.
The aliens can't open it,
but soon work out a plan...

They place a shiny rock in front,
then hide behind the door.
These astronauts all LOVE new
rocks, so race out to explore!

Each astronaut is suddenly
    tipped upside down and shaken.
Landing on their heads, they find
    their boots have just been taken!

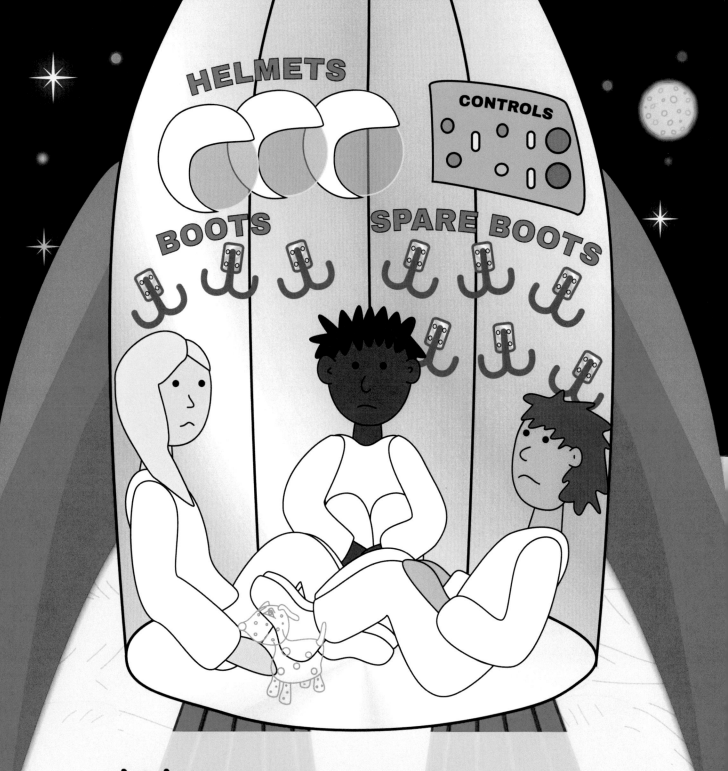

"**W**e've had ENOUGH of aliens!"
the astronauts declare.
"With ALL our boots now stolen,
we have nothing left to wear!"

The spaceship zooms straight home,
with all its booster rockets burning.
The astronauts are certain
that they'll NEVER be returning!

Look! Another spaceship!
What a WONDERFUL surprise!
It's been so long, the aliens
can't quite believe their eyes!

To try to wake their friends, they
give the spaceship a good shake.
They can't see ANY astronauts -
there must be some mistake!

A shiny rock is placed outside,
to see what happens next.
The spaceship starts to WALK –
which leaves the aliens perplexed!

They gasp, as from the door appears
a long and bendy trunk!
The rock is sucked up whole, then
swallowed down in one big chunk!

Suddenly they hear a voice...
Did THAT come out of THERE?
The aliens are curious;
they stand around and stare.

They name this creature "Hi", as
that's the first thing that he said.
He's invited to their village, where
they make their guest a bed.

When it's time to eat, they
feed him lots of shiny rocks.
"Hi" gives their king a present –
silver boots, wrapped in a box!

"Hi" starts to go to school, where
he is taught his "Zop, Zep, Zees";
Then he teaches all the children
his odd-sounding A, B, Cs.

The kids all love to play with "Hi",
and collect him rocks to eat.
Some days he hands red BOOTS out,
as a special lunchtime treat!

"Hi" tells them he's a robot, who
was sent from Earth to learn.
His fuel ran out while getting
here, so now he can't return.

Zippety and Zoppety
did not like going to school,
But now that "Hi" has joined them,
they both think that learning's cool!

They know poor "Hi" is sad, though,
as he wants to go back home;
So they show him the great project
in their father's, secret dome...

This spaceship is GIGANTIC,
though has not yet managed flight.
Their Dad has tried his best, but
there is something not quite right...

Ermm...

"Hi" looks at all the diagrams;
he soon spots what is wrong.
He has the twins to help him -
the repairs will not take long.

This spaceship runs on rocks,
and so, with some refueling stops,
"Hi" SHOULD reach home on Earth
again in just two hundred hops!

"Hi" gives out boots to all his friends,
and sheds some oily tears,
Then sets off on a lengthy voyage,
that may take several years.

This time he WON'T be on his own.
Inside that great big ship,
Sit the twins and both their parents,
looking forward to their trip!

So, IF you spot a spaceship land,
with unexpected guests,
Don't be surprised if BOOTS should
be the first of their requests!

The Top of the Wardrobe Gang

This group of cuddly toys work as a team to write their own books. They live on top of Billy's wardrobe (which they call the "Penthouse Suite").

You can find out lots more about them from their website at

http://topofthewardrobegang.weebly.com

Billy
(their human owner)

Odd Sock
(colors in big bits)

Oscar Rabbit
(in charge)

Burton Bear
(writes)

P. D. Monkey
(draws)

Terry Tiger
(colors in
small bits)

Buster Dog
(Collects and
delivers mail)

Melinda - friend of
Billy's Mom
(helps put everything
together)

Alien Puzzles

1. Shadow Matching

Can you match these aliens
to their shadows?

A **B** **C** **D**

1 **2** **3** **4**

2. Outer Space Maze

Can you help this spaceship find its way to Earth?

3. Spot the Difference

Can you spot six differences between these two pictures?

4. Tangled String

Can you follow the tangled string to see
which alien gets which color of boot?
Do any get their favorite boot?

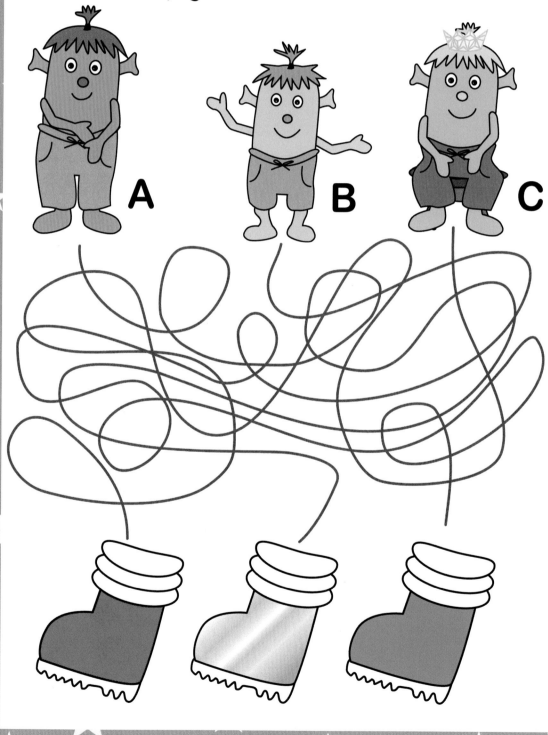

5. Which Two Are the Same?

Can you spot which two of these pictures of Zog are identical?

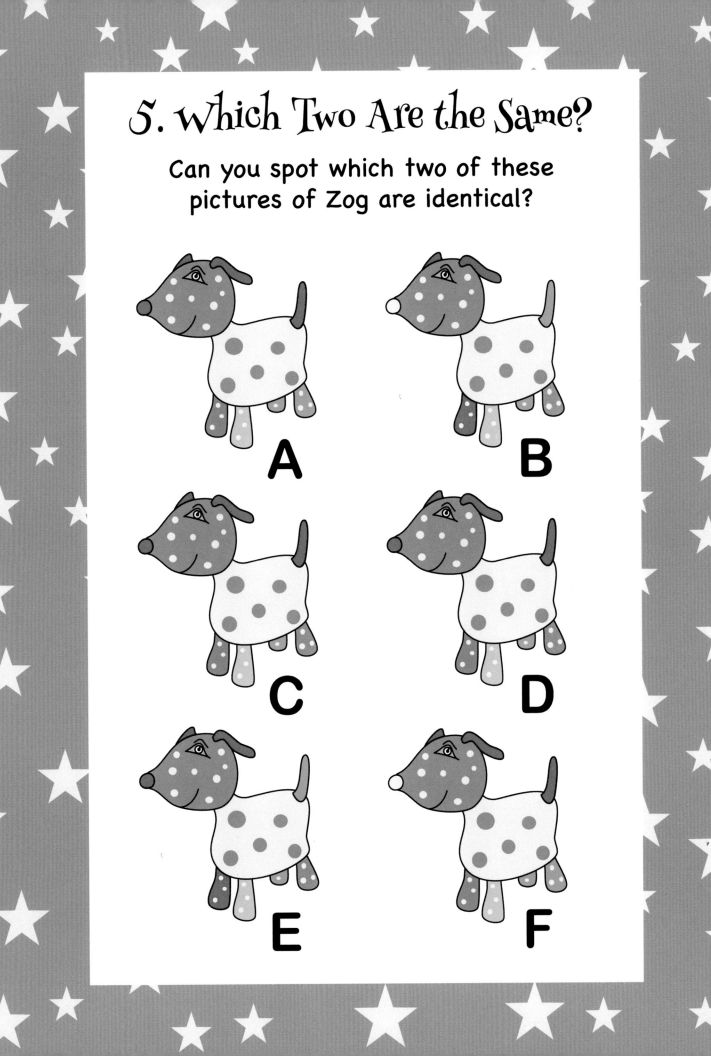

A

B

C

D

E

F

6. Crossword Puzzle

Can you use the pictures to fill in the answers
to this crossword puzzle? The first letter
of each word is already given.

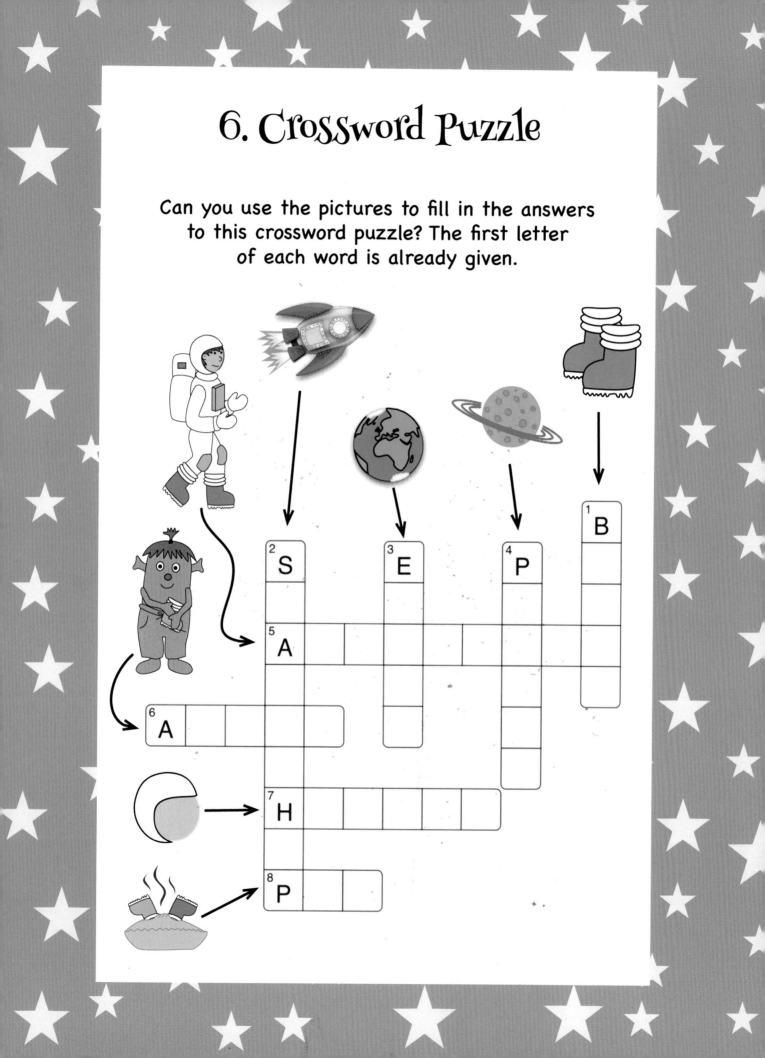

7. Color In Zoppety

Why not use your pencils or crayons
to color in the young alien twin Zoppety?

Alien Puzzle Answers

2. Outer Space Maze

6. Crossword Puzzle

									¹B
²S		³E		⁴P					O
P		A		L					O
⁵A	S	T	R	O	N	A	U	T	S
C		H		A					
⁶A	L	I	E	N					
S				E					
⁷H	E	L	M	E	T				
I									
⁸P	I	E							

1. Shadow Matching

Alien A's shadow is 3, B's is 4, C's is 2 and D's is 1.

3. Spot the Difference

The six differences between the two pictures are that in the bottom picture:

1. There are no rings around the orange planet.
2. The alien on the far left now holds a red boot and a blue one instead of 2 blue boots.
3. The badge on the female astronaut's pack is blue not red.
4. You can't see the astronaut in the spaceship's head through the window.
5. There is a white star missing from below the purple and blue planets.
6. The alien on the far right has no tied bunch of hair on top of his head.

4. Tangled String

Alien A gets silver boots; B gets blue; C gets silver. (No alien gets their favorite.)

5. Which 2 are the same?

Zogs C and D are identical.

We hope you enjoyed our book, and that we'll see you again soon.

Bye for now!

From
The Top of the Wardrobe Gang

Other books...

Amazon links to all of the Top of the Wardrobe Gang
books can easily be found on our website at
http://topofthewardrobegang.weebly.com,
or by typing "Melinda Kinsman"
into the Amazon search box.

So far, we have written the following Rhyming
Picture Books / Beginner Readers for ages 3-7...

The following Beginner Reader Books for ages 3+...

And the following Early Chapterbooks for ages 5-8...

Made in the USA
Middletown, DE
05 December 2016